Super Sidekick:
The Musical

Book by Gregory Crafts

Music and Lyrics by
Michael Gordon Shapiro

A SAMUEL FRENCH ACTING EDITION

SAMUELFRENCH.COM

RENTAL MATERIALS

An orchestration consisting of **Piano/Conductor's Score** and parts for **Piano, Guitar, Bass, Drums** and **Vocal/Chorus Books; Instrumental Tracks; and Demo Recording Audio Tracks** will be loaned two months prior to the production ONLY on the receipt of the Licensing Fee quoted for all performances, the rental fee and a refundable deposit.

Please contact Samuel French for perusal of the music materials as well as a performance license application.

IMPORTANT BILLING AND CREDIT
REQUIREMENTS

All producers of *SUPER SIDEKICK must* give credit to the Authors of the Play in all programs distributed in connection with performances of the Play, and in all instances in which the title of the Play appears for the purposes of advertising, publicizing or otherwise exploiting the Play and/or a production. The name of the Authors *must* appear on a separate line on which no other name appears, immediately following the title and *must* appear in size of type not less than fifty percent of the size of the title type.

SUPER SIDEKICK had its world premiere at Sherry Theatre in North Hollywood, CA on July 18th, 2010 as part of the 3rd Annual Los Angeles Festival of New American Musicals (www.lafestival.org). It was produced by Theatre Unleashed and directed by Jenn Scuderi. Choreography was by Jessica Brusilow, and the fight choreographers were Sean Fitzgerald and Robyn Heller. The stage manager was Erin Scott. The cast was as follows:

INKY . . . . .Scott Sharma

BLACKJACK. . . . . Jase Lindgren

SORCERER SLURM. . . . . Mark Anthony Lopez

PRINCESS PENELOPE . . . . Hannah Nawroth

QUEEN/NARRATOR/MRS. APPLEBAUM/MONSTER. . . . . . .Robyn Heller

NINJA KOALA/MONSTER/CITIZEN 1 . . . . .Lindsey Moore Ford

NINJA KOALA/MONSTER/MS. SMITH/CITIZEN 2. . . Sara-Beth Wichman

SUPER SIDEKICK was produced by Theatre Unleashed, as part of the Hollywood Fringe Festival, in Los Angeles, California in June, 2011. The performance was directed by Jenn Scuderi with choreography by Ana Therese Lopez. The fight choreographer was Sean Fitzgerald. The stage manager was Erin Scott. The cast was as follows:

INKY . . . . .Scott Sharma

BLACKJACK. . . . . Noah Butler

SORCERER SLURM. . . . . .Shawn Cahill

PRINCESS PENELOPE . . . . Hannah Nawroth

QUEEN/NINJA KOALA. . . . . Heather Lake

NINJA KOALA/CITIZEN . . . . Ana Therese Lopez

NINJA KOALA/CITIZEN . . . . .Sara-BethWichman

NINJA KOALA/CITIZEN . . . . .Jude Evans

SUPER SIDEKICK was given a "Best of Fringe" extended run with Theatre Unleashed, in Los Angeles, California in September, 2011. The director was Jenn Scuderi with choreography by Ana Therese Lopez. The fight choreographer was Sean Fitzgerald. The stage manager was Erin Scott. The cast was as follows:

INKY . . . . .Scott Sharma

BLACKJACK. . . . . .Jude Evans

SORCERER SLURM. . . . . .Shawn Cahill

PRINCESS PENELOPE . . . . Kailey Nicole Swanson

QUEEN/NINJA KOALA. . . . . Heather Lake

NINJA KOALA . . . . Ana Therese Lopez

NINJA KOALA . . . . .Katelin Han

NINJA KOALA . . . . .Beth Wallan

CHARACTERS

INKY – Sidekick to a famous superhero. Youthful.

BLACKJACK THE BOLD – A famous and somewhat self-absorbed superhero.

PRINCESS PENELOPE – A princess about Inky's age, with a fiery independent streak.

SORCERER SLURM – The villain. More inept than truly scary.

CITIZEN 1/BLUE NINJA KOALA/MONSTER – Swing

CITIZEN 2/PINK NINJA KOALA/MONSTER – Swing

CITIZEN 3/SPECTATOR/MR. SMITH/MONSTER – Swing

CITIZEN 4/MRS. APPLEBAUM/THE QUEEN/MONSTER – Swing

SCENE SYNOPSIS

PROLOGUE

SCENE I: Outside the Courthouse

SCENE II: The Trial & Escape from the Throne Room

SCENE III: Going it Alone

SCENE IV: Blackjack and the Cave of Doom

SCENE V: Outside the Cave of Doom

SCENE VI: Don't Feed the Bears

SCENE VII: The Princess Escapes

SCENE VIII: It's Hard to Be Evil

SCENE IX: The Final Encounter – Part 1

SCENE X: The Final Encounter – Part 2

EPILOGUE

Average Running Time: 1 hour

PROPERTIES LIST

Narrator's Storybook

Notes (ransom-style)

Eucalyptus Leaves

Coconut Medallion with Crossed Licorice Bars

Terrible Ticklers (three large feathers on sticks or

rods sturdy enough for stage combat)

Big Rock

Giant Red Push-Button

Manacles

Signs that say "DO NOT TOUCH" and "MANACLE RELEASE"

MUSIC PRODUCTION NOTE

Super Sidekick's score is meant to be accessible to production companies with generous and modest music budgets alike. Music may be performed live by musicians, or via the included pre-recorded accompaniment tracks.

For live music production, a full set of parts and scores are provided. Piano is obligatory; the other instruments (guitar, drums, and bass) can be added in any combination. Enterprising music directors can also make use of the chord charts and incorporate instruments not part of the "official" specification.

The pre-recorded tracks are a great option when musicians aren't available. They even provide one distinct advantage: the arrangements in the pre-records are often larger than the live versions, incorporating orchestral ensembles as well as expanded rhythm sections. In a nutshell, both approaches have their own strengths. Pick whichever option best suits the style and resources of your production company.

UNDERSCORE NOTE

The instrumental underscore cues provide additional excitement and dramatic meaning to key story moments. Like the vocal songs, underscore can be performed live or via playback of included prerecorded tracks.

MUSICAL NUMBERS

"Blackjack!" (2:30) . . . . **BLACKJACK, INKY, CHORUS**

"If I Were a Hero Too" (3:51) . . . . **INKY, MRS. APPLEBAUM**

"The Caves of Doom" (3:07) . . . . **INKY, MONSTER CHORUS**

"Inky and the Princess" (2:36) . . . . **INKY, PRINCESS PENELOPE**

"Slurm's Soliloquy" (3:50) . . . . **SORCERER SLURM, NINJA KOALAS**

"The Final Encounter – Part 1" (1:10) . . . . . **PRINCESS PENELOPE, INKY**

"The Final Encounter – Part 2" (1:05) . . . . **SORCERER SLURM**

"Super Finale" (0:52) . . . . **ENSEMBLE**

The "Chorus" consists of all available actors who make sense for the scene.
The actor playing Slurm is ideally omitted from the opening chorus so as
to save his reveal for later.

MUSIC UNDERSCORE CUES

"Once Upon a Time"

"Koala Attack"

"Night Falls"

"The Princess Escapes"

"Super Heroes Away!"

"Terrible Tickler Fanfare"

"Battle With Slurm"

"Happily Ever After"

PRERECORDS AND VAMPS NOTE

Certain underscore cues provide vamps (repeated passages) to accommo-
date the uncertain timing of onstage events. Live musicians can simply
repeat the vamps as needed until actors reach the cue for the next section.
The pre-recorded tracks are in these cases split into pairs, corresponding
to before and after the vamp section. The vamp passage is repeated sev-
eral times at the end of each "before" track. The stage manager or sound
designer can interrupt the vamp cycle and advance to the next music track
at the appropriate moment.

MUSIC ELEMENTS IN STORY ORDER

1. UNDERSCORE – "Once Upon a Time"

2. SONG – "Blackjack!"

3. UNDERSCORE – "Koala Attack"

4. UNDERSCORE – "Night Falls"

5. SONG – "If I Were a Hero Too"

6. SONG – "The Caves of Doom"

7. UNDERSCORE – "The Princess Escapes"

8. SONG – "Inky and the Princess"

9. UNDERSCORE – "Super Heroes Away!"

10. UNDERSCORE – "Terrible Tickler Fanfare"

11. SONG – "Slurm's Soliloquy"

12. UNDERSCORE – "Terrible Tickler Fanfare" (repeated)

13. SONG – "The Final Encounter - Part 1"

14. SONG – "The Final Encounter - Part 2"

15. UNDERSCORE – "Terrible Tickler Fanfare" (interrupted)

16. UNDERSCORE – "Battle With Slurm"

17. UNDERSCORE – "Happily Ever After"

18. SONG – "Super Finale"

PROLOGUE

*(The prologue begins in darkness. The **NARRATOR** sits stage right with a large storybook cradled in her lap. She opens it and begins to read aloud.)*

*(MUSIC: "**ONCE UPON A TIME**" [underscore])*

NARRATOR. This story begins just as many good stories do: Once upon a time, in a land far, far away, there was a boy named Inky.

*(Enter **INKY**.)*

Inky was a sidekick. Not just any old kind of sidekick, though; a super sidekick! Inky was sidekick to the greatest superhero of the land, Blackjack the Bold!

*(Enter **BLACKJACK**.)*

Inky wanted to be a superhero just like Blackjack. To become one though, he had a lot to learn. Like how to toss his hair heroically, or wear a cape without getting it caught in an escalator. Blackjack agreed to teach Inky how to be a hero, and from that day on, they did everything together.

*(**INKY** and **BLACKJACK** pantomime the following activities. At every opportunity, **BLACKJACK** upstages and overshadows **INKY**, who is too naïve to realize the inequity of the situation.)*

They played together, did chores together and, most importantly, fought evil together. Fighting evil is what they did best. They captured the Cookie Chomping Culprit, defeated the Devious Devil Fish and beat the Bobble Head Bandit. Together, they were unstoppable. They saved the Kingdom more times than you can count on your fingers AND your toes! However, the greatest challenge the daring duo would ever face was yet to come.

(The scene shifts. The **NARRATOR** *stands up, closes the storybook and moves offstage.)*

SCENE I

(Outside the Castle. A hustle and bustle on the stage. **CITIZENS** *of the Kingdom enter and mill about. They're excited.)*

CITIZEN 1. Is it true about Slurm? Did they catch him?

CITIZEN 2. I think so. They're bringing him here now!

CITIZEN 1. Who's bringing him?

CITIZEN 3. Blackjack the Bold!

(SFX: "BLACKJACK'S CHIME" [This may be a chime sound effect, a high note played on the piano, etc.])

(All characters onstage pause for a beat and give the audience a large, superheroic, toothy smile.)

And his sidekick.

CITIZEN 4. Blackjack's coming here?!? When!?!

CITIZEN 2. Now, I think! The Queen's going to put Slurm on trial.

CITIZEN 1. Wha'd he do now?

CITIZEN 3. He was trying to cover the streets in rotten banana peels so everyone would trip and fall.

CITIZEN 1. That's just nasty.

CITIZEN 2. And gross, too!

CITIZEN 4. Yeah, thank goodness Blackjack stopped him!

CITIZEN 3. I hear the Princess is coming down to see the trial.

CITIZEN 2. Princess Penelope?

CITIZEN 4. The one and only.

CITIZEN 1. Wow, this is a big day for the Kingdom!

CITIZEN 3. Yeah! No kidding! She's so pretty!

CITIZEN 2. *(looking off)* Is that him? Is that Blackjack?

CITIZEN 4. Where?

CITIZEN 3. There!

CITIZEN 1. I think so!

CITIZEN 2. It's him! He's coming! He's coming!

*(Everyone gets excited and huddles together, staring, awaiting the entrance of the heroes. Music starts. They start to raise a cheer as…**INKY**, the humble sidekick, enters. The cheer quickly deflates.)*

CITIZEN 4. Aww…it's just the sidekick.

CITIZEN 3. Yeah, what's his name? Blinky?

CITIZEN 2. Stinky?

INKY. Inky.

CITIZEN 1. No, that's not it.

INKY. Guys, it's Inky. That's my name.

CITIZEN 4. Whatever. You're just the sidekick anyway. Where's Blackjack?

CITIZEN 3. Yeah! Where's Blackjack? We want a real Superhero!

*(The crowd of **CITIZENS** all start to bustle and swarm around **INKY**, demanding to know where Blackjack is. Suddenly, **BLACKJACK** jumps onstage.)*

*(MUSIC: "**BLACKJACK!**")*

BLACKJACK.
I'M IN!
I HEAR YOU NEED A BIT OF RESCUIN'
BY SOMEONE BOLDER OR STRONGER
OKAY!
PERHAPS YOU'RE LOOKING FOR SOME MONSTER-SLAYIN'?
OR SOME SAVE-THE-DAYIN'?
WELL WAIT NO LONGER!

'CAUSE HELP'S A-COMIN' AND FOES ARE RUNNING
'CAUSE THEY DON'T STACK AGAINST BLACKJACK
I'LL SAVE THE DAY, SEND THE CREEPS AWAY
AND DISPLAY MY STYLISH TAN
'CAUSE A HERO'S HERE, OH YEAH

IT'S ME!
I'LL SAVE YOUR KITTENS FROM THE TALLEST TREES
REALLY, IT'S A BREEZE, NOT A PROBLEM
GET DOWN!
I'LL WRESTLE HUNGRY DRAGONS TO THE GROUND

OR FIGHT ANY GIANT OR GOBLIN

I'LL MOP THE FLOOR WITH THE DEMON CORPS
IF YOU'VE CRIME IN STORE, WATCH YOUR BACK, JACK
I'LL SAVE THE WORLD AND CHARM ALL THE GIRLS
AND FORGET ABOUT SUPERMAN! (PTUI!)
'CAUSE A HERO'S HERE, OH YEAH

SO MANY PEOPLE SING MY SONG
AND ALL THOSE PEOPLE CAN'T BE WRONG
AND REST ASSURED, I'D UNDERSTAND
IF YOU SHOULD SWOON OR KISS MY HAND
AS I GO FORTH TO TAKE MY STAND
TO SEE WHAT PROVIDENCE HAS PLANNED
TO SEE WHAT DESTINY HAS GOT IN STORE FOR ME
WHAT FATEFULNESS OF FATE
DRAWS NEAR AND/OR AWAITS…

(confused)

Uh…what was I saying?

INKY. You're great?

BLACKJACK. *(wakes up)* I'm great!

CHORUS.

HE'S GREAT!
HE'S THE HERO ALL THE VILLAINS HATE!

BLACKJACK.

'CAUSE THEY KNOW I'M THE LATEST SENSATION

CHORUS.

BAR NONE!
HE'LL BATTLE EVIL 'TIL THE BATTLE'S WON!

BLACKJACK.

AND I'M FUN AT FORMAL OCCASIONS

BLACKJACK AND CHORUS.

NOW HELP'S A-COMIN' AND THUGS ARE RUNNING
'CAUSE THEY DON'T STACK AGAINST BLACKJACK

BLACKJACK.

I'LL SOLVE THE CRIME, AND BE BACK IN TIME
TO SIGN SOME PICTURES FOR ADORING FANS

(Girls in the chorus swoon.)

BLACKJACK. *(cont.)*
'CAUSE A HERO'S HERE...
INKY. Blackjack, I think we're late!
BLACKJACK AND CHORUS.
OH YEAH!

SCENE II

*(The scene shifts behind **INKY** and **BLACKJACK**. Enter the **QUEEN** and the **PRINCESS**. **INKY** and **BLACKJACK** wait off to the side for **SLURM**, who enters bound in chains. The two heroes escort him to his final position onstage. **INKY** spies the **PRINCESS**.)*

INKY. There's Princess Penelope! Wow, she's even prettier than I imagined…

*(**INKY** waves shyly to the **PRINCESS**. The **PRINCESS** blows a kiss to the heroes. **INKY** looks like he's about to catch it, when **BLACKJACK** snatches the kiss out of thin air as if it was meant for him all along.)*

BLACKJACK. C'mon Inky, the trial's about to start.

*(**INKY** is dejected. Nevertheless, the heroes assume their positions in the courtroom. **INKY** on the witness stand and **BLACKJACK** in front of him as the Prosecutor. When they settle, the trial begins.)*

QUEEN. Sorcerer Slurm, you are here on trial for crimes against the Kingdom, including treason, sabotage, kidnapping, and wearing a bad moustache. What is your plea?

SLURM. Not guilty. I have a very nice moustache.

QUEEN. Blackjack the Bold…

(SFX: "Blackjack's Chime")

*(All adult characters onstage, including **SLURM**, turn to the audience for a beat and give a large, toothy grin. **INKY** and the **PRINCESS** don't notice.)*

…you may examine your witness.

SLURM. I object! This witness is biased!

QUEEN. Is this true, Blackjack?

BLACKJACK. Absolutely not, your Highness. I can personally guarantee that the witness is impartial.

QUEEN. How can you be certain?

BLACKJACK. He's my sidekick.

QUEEN. Oh, alright then. I'll allow it.

BLACKJACK. *(to* **INKY,** *whispered)* Okay Inky, just remember to say exactly what I told you earlier, okay?

INKY. Yes.

(**BLACKJACK** *turns to* **INKY** *and begins to grill him.)*

BLACKJACK. Inky, two days ago, did you see Sorcerer Slurm try to do something?

INKY. Yes.

BLACKJACK. Was it evil?

INKY. Yes.

BLACKJACK. Did you see Slurm try to spread rotten banana peels all over the Kingdom's streets so people would slip and fall?

INKY. Yes.

BLACKJACK. Did you see me, Blackjack the Bold…

(SFX: "Blackjack's Chime")

(The adults onstage turn to the audience for a beat and give them a large, toothy grin. **INKY** *and the* **PRINCESS** *don't notice.)*

…stop Slurm's evil plot in the nick of time and capture him, saving the day and the Kingdom from certain rotten, slippery doom?

INKY. *(beat)* Yes.

BLACKJACK. *(to* **QUEEN***)* The Prosecution rests. *(to* **INKY***)* Well done. You may step down.

INKY. Yes.

(**BLACKJACK** *shoots* **INKY** *a glare.* **INKY** *and* **BLACKJACK** *walk together to the side of the throne room and watch the* **QUEEN** *hand down the verdict.)*

QUEEN. Sorcerer Slurm, you have been found guilty of all charges. Before we sentence you, do you have anything to say for yourself?

SLURM. Why yes, Queen. Yes, I do.

(**NINJA KOALAS** *tumble into the room!*)

(*MUSIC: "**KOALA ATTACK**" [underscore]*)

YOU'LL NEVER STOP ME! MUHUAHAHAHAH!!!

(*One* **KOALA** *jumps at* **BLACKJACK** *and throws* **BLACKJACK**'s *cape over his eyes, then moves to* **SLURM** *and undoes his chains.* **BLACKJACK** *stumbles around blindly. Another* **KOALA** *engages* **INKY**. **BLACKJACK** *is still fumbling with his cape, but* **INKY** *is holding his own against the* **KOALA**. *Once* **SLURM** *is freed, he grabs the* **PRINCESS**. *The second* **KOALA** *joins in the fray against* **INKY**, *but before you know it, both* **KOALAS** *find themselves grappled by* **INKY**. *All is saved! Until, that is,* **SLURM** *shoves the still-blind* **BLACKJACK** *into* **INKY**. *The* **KOALAS** *get up and the villains exit, kidnapping the* **PRINCESS**. *After a beat,* **INKY** *and* **BLACKJACK** *untangle themselves.* **BLACKJACK** *finally manages to remove his cape from his face.*)

BLACKJACK. Inky! What happened?!? I had them right where I wanted them!

QUEEN. Slurm has escaped and taken my daughter, the Princess! This is terrible! How could you let this happen?

BLACKJACK. I'm sorry, your Highness. He had Ninja teddy bears with him. They're very dangerous, you know. But don't worry. Inky and I have everything under control. We'll rescue the Princess and recapture Slurm.

QUEEN. But how? You don't even know where they've gone!

(**BLACKJACK** *is about to say something, but pauses, at a loss for words. Suddenly, a ball wrapped in paper soars onstage and hits* **INKY** *in the head.*)

INKY. OW!

BLACKJACK. Don't worry, your Highness. We'll think of something.

(**INKY** *picks up the ball.*)

BLACKJACK. *(cont.)* Inky, leave that alone. We'll have time to clean up the litter later. Right now we have to find Slurm and save the Princess.

(**INKY** *removes the paper from the ball.*)

INKY. Hey, it's a note!

BLACKJACK. Never mind about that Inky, I'm trying to think!

(**INKY** *reads from the note.*)

INKY. "Dear Half-Wit Heroes. I have taken the Prin–"

(**BLACKJACK** *realizes what* **INKY** *is holding and grabs the note from him.*)

BLACKJACK. "Dear Half-Wit Heroes. I have taken the Princess to my Super Secret Lair where I intend to test my latest Evil Invention upon her. Then, I will take over the Kingdom, and not even you two fools can stop me. Don't even try to find us. You won't. My lair is too super and too secret for you to ever find it. Really. I mean it. MUHUHAHAHA– *(flips the note, continues)* –HAHAHAHA!!! Signed, Sorcerer Slurm. Caves of Doom, Suite 7. The Kingdom."

(**BLACKJACK** *tosses the note away.*)

Oh no! He does have the Princess! And a new Evil Invention! And we'll never find him! We're doomed!

(**INKY** *picks up the discarded note and reads it.*)

INKY. Uh, Blackjack?

BLACKJACK. It's too late! We should evacuate the Kingdom! Head for the hills! Run! Hide! Disaster is coming!

INKY. Blackjack....

BLACKJACK. The world is ending! Save yourselves!

INKY. Blackjack! *(beat)* I think I know where Slurm is.

BLACKJACK. How could you know? We can never find him! He said so!

INKY. I know, but I think he's in the Caves of Doom.

BLACKJACK. Oh yeah? *(laughs)* Well, how do you know that, Mr. Smarty Sidekick?

INKY. Because it says here in the note.

> *(Beat.* **BLACKJACK** *grabs the note from* **INKY** *and reads it again. Beat.* **BLACKJACK** *then rolls it up and bonks* **INKY** *on the head with it.)*

BLACKJACK. Of course Slurm's in the Caves of Doom! I told you we'd find him. What are you so upset about?

INKY. I'm sorry, Blackjack.

BLACKJACK. That's right. *(turns to* **QUEEN***)* Your Highness, never fear. I'll get the Princess back and recapture Slurm and bring him back here to stand trial.

QUEEN. Oh, thank you Blackjack!

> *(***BLACKJACK*** *gets ready to leave and strikes a "getting ready to fly" stance.)*

BLACKJACK. Blackjack the Bold...

> *(SFX: "Blackjack's Chime")*

> *(The adults onstage turn to the audience for a beat and give them a large, toothy grin.* **INKY** *doesn't notice.)*

...away!

> *(***INKY*** *is left in the dust.)*

INKY. Hey Blackjack! Wait for me! *(***INKY*** *strikes his own stance.)* Super Sidekick Inky, away!

SCENE III

(Outside the entrance to the Caves of Doom. **BLACKJACK** *enters, with* **INKY** *coming on a beat after him.)*

INKY. *(cont.)* Hey Blackjack! Blackjack! Wait up!

*(***BLACKJACK*** stops and turns around.)*

BLACKJACK. What?

INKY. Well, what's the plan? We going to go get 'em and hit Slurm and those Ninja Koalas with the ol' One-Two, or do you want to use the new One-Two-Three?

BLACKJACK. No, Inky. I'm going by myself.

INKY. What?

BLACKJACK. Just like I told the Queen, I'm going to the Caves of Doom, stopping Slurm and rescuing the Princess myself.

INKY. Well, just because you told the Queen you'd do it yourself doesn't mean you have to.

BLACKJACK. Inky, that's not the point. I'm going to fight Slurm alone.

INKY. And you want me to save the Princess. Right! Teamwork!

BLACKJACK. No, that's not what I meant. You couldn't handle two overgrown teddy bears–

INKY. I think they're koala bears, actually.

BLACKJACK. Whatever! You couldn't even handle two koala bears in colored pajamas by yourself. How can I expect you to try and help me save the Kingdom? This is a job for a hero! Not a sidekick!

INKY. But Blackjack, every hero needs a sidekick. You'll need help!

BLACKJACK. I don't need help in there, Inky! Especially from you!

(beat)

INKY. So, you'll need my help out here, then?

BLACKJACK. No! *(realizes what* **INKY** *has said)* I mean, yes! Yes! I do need your help, Inky! I have a job that's perfect for a Super Sidekick.

(guides **INKY** *to a spot near the cave entrance)*

I need you to stand right here on this spot and keep watch for snipes.

INKY. What's a snipe?

BLACKJACK. A snipe is a rare and special bird that is invisible to grown-up superheroes. It is vitally important that they all be counted. You see why I must leave this task to you.

INKY. I guess…

BLACKJACK. *(swiveling* **INKY** *to face out to the audience)* Snipes are usually seen over that horizon, there. So keep watching that spot. Only you can do this, Inky!

*(***BLACKJACK*** starts to exit.)*

INKY. *(turning to face the the retreating* **BLACKJACK***)* Blackjack?

*(***BLACKJACK*** stops.)*

BLACKJACK. What is it, Inky?

INKY. What if I have to go to the bathroom?

BLACKJACK. I'll be back before you have to go to the bathroom.

INKY. Okay.

*(***BLACKJACK*** again starts to exit.)*

Blackjack?

*(***BLACKJACK*** stops.)*

BLACKJACK. What?!?

INKY. What if it gets dark?

BLACKJACK. *(gritting his teeth)* I will definitely be back before it gets dark. Okay?

(Without waiting for an answer, **BLACKJACK** *turns around and practically runs offstage.)*

INKY. Blackjack! *(turns around and sees that* **BLACKJACK** *has left)* Blackjack? *(beat)* He's gone. *(beat, then, trying to rally his confidence)* Okay! See you soon! I'll keep watch out for snipes! See you before it gets dark!

*(MUSIC: "**NIGHT FALLS**" [underscore])*

(Abruptly the lights dim and we hear the sound of crickets, wolves, and other night wildlife. **INKY***'s eyes go wide.)*

(Blackout)

SCENE IV

(**BLACKJACK** *sticks his head onstage.*)

BLACKJACK. At last! The Caves of Doom. Hmm…it's dark in there. (**BLACKJACK** *turns back and looks at where* **INKY** *usually stands.*) Inky, how about you scou– Inky? Inky? Oh yeah, he's not here. I guess I'll just have to go in myself. (**BLACKJACK** *stands right at the entrance to the cave.*) Hello? (*He listens to his voice echo.*) Oh well, I don't see anyone. I guess no one's home. I'll just come back another time then.

(*He turns to leave, but suddenly hears a roar behind him.* **BLACKJACK** *dives into the cave to hide.*)

Gah! What was that?!?

(**BLACKJACK** *looks in terror outside the cave but sees nothing. He suddenly realizes where he is.*) Gah! It's dark in here!!! Oh, I HATE the dark! I mean, it's scary, isn't it? Oh well, since I'm already in here, I may as well see if the Princess is in here. Princess? Hellooo?? (**BLACKJACK** *starts to go deeper into the cave.*) Wow, this is a deep cave. (*He pauses and plays to the audience to fill in the sound effects for the next part.*) Wait! Did you hear that?!? It sounded like a hissing sound! And that! A growl! And that! A squeak! Gah! (*He starts to back out of the cave.*) Oh, I hate the dark, I hate the dark, I hate the dark, I hate the dark.

(*As he nears the entrance to the cave,* **NINJA KOALAS** *enter, silently.* **BLACKJACK** *backs into them and turns around. They strike a fighting stance and yell. He looks at them, turns to the audience, screams like a little girl and faints dead away into their arms. The* **NINJA KOALAS** *shrug and drag him off.*)

SCENE V

*(Outside the Caves of Doom. **INKY** is just as he said he would be; still standing in the field waiting for **BLACKJACK** to return.)*

INKY. Wow, Blackjack's sure taking a long time. I hope everything's okay. Slurm's pretty dangerous. Oh, of course he's okay. Blackjack is the greatest superhero ever! He's the strongest, he's the fastest and he's the most attractive! At least, that's what he always tells me…

(Time passes.)

It's dark and Blackjack's not back yet, and I haven't seen a single snipe. I feel like I've let down the Queen and the birdwatching community too. *(beat)* Oooohhhhh… why do I need to stay here and hunt for a snipe? Huh? I mean, the Princess is in trouble! That's far more important! How am I going to ever be a full superhero if I can never take part in the real missions!? If I'm…

*(MUSIC: **"IF I WERE A HERO TOO"**)*

INKY.

ALWAYS LEFT BEHIND
ALWAYS STUCK ON THE SIDELINES, JUST A GUARD
WHEN THINGS GET TOUGH, WHEN THINGS GET HARD
I'M TOLD TO STEP ASIDE
I GUESS I UNDERSTAND
I'M JUST A SIDEKICK, AFTER ALL
NOT VERY DARING, SMART, OR TALL
NOBODY WHO COULD TURN THE TIDE

BUT WHAT I WOULDN'T GIVE TO BE
ASKED TO COME ALONG
ASKED TO LEND A HAND
ALLOWED TO RISK A FALL
ALLOWED TO TAKE A STAND
IF THEY JUST LET ME TRY, THEY'D SEE

BUT I GUESS
THERE'S NO POINT IN WONDERING WHAT I'D DO
IF I WERE A HERO TOO
THERE'S NO POINT
IT'S JUST CONJECTURE
SO I WON'T THINK ABOUT IT

(*Beat.* **INKY** *suddenly leaps to his feet, electrified with imagination.*)

I WOULD RACE THROUGH THE NIGHT
PATROLLING EACH CITY AND STREET
EVER DILIGENT, EVER VIGILANT
NOTHING ESCAPING MY VIEW
I'D PERFORM MIGHTY FEATS
RESCUING DAMSELS AND BATTLING JERKS
IT'D BE PART OF A GOOD DAY'S WORK
IF I WERE A HERO TOO
SOME MIGHT NOT KNOW MY NAME
BUT I'D DEFEND THEM JUST THE SAME
'CAUSE IT'S RIGHT! AND IT'S GOOD!
AND THE COMIC BOOKS STRONGLY IMPLY THAT I SHOULD!
AND THOSE WHO SHAKE IN FEAR
WILL SHAKE NO MORE WHEN I AM HERE!
…I MEAN THERE!
…I'LL FIGURE THIS OUT, AND WHEN I DO EVIL HAD BETTER
   BEWARE!
AND THAT'S JUST THE START OF ALL THAT I'D DO
IF I WERE A HERO TOO!
When all seemed peaceful, I'd walk among the people of the kingdom, concealed by my secret identity!

(**INKY** *enacts a scene from his imagined life. Making his rounds, he briefly interacts with various* **CITIZENS OF THE KINGDOM** [**MR. SMITH** *and* **MRS. APPLEBAUM**].)

MR. SMITH. Oh hi, Inky!

INKY. Hi Mister Smith! What are you up to today?

MR. SMITH. Oh, nothing, just tending the garden. You?

INKY. Just enjoying a walk. Not leading the fight against evil in any way! Ha ha!

MRS. APPLEBAUM. Inky!

INKY. Hello, Mrs. Applebaum!

MRS. APPLEBAUM. I saw smoke rising from your basement yesterday. You wouldn't happen to be constructing a superphotonic modulatory energy condenser for use in laying siege to villainous fortresses, would you?

(Music pauses. Beat.)

INKY. Uh…no?

(Music resumes.)

MRS. APPLEBAUM. Oh. My mistake! Have a nice day, sweetie.

INKY. Phew, that was close!

(He resumes singing.)

I'D BATTLE GOBLIN HORDES
AND EVIL GHOULS WITH EVIL WARDS
I WOULD SHINE!
I'D TAKE A STAND AGAINST LITTER AND CUTTING IN LINE!
I'D KEEP WATCH ON THE SKIES
KNOWING THAT EVIL NEVER LIES!
… I MEAN, LIES DOWN!
… IT LIES ALL THE TIME! BUT THAT'S WHY I'D BE AROUND!
AND WHEN I'M FULLY GROWN
I'LL HAVE A SIDEKICK OF MY OWN!
AND HE'LL…

NEVER BE LEFT BEHIND
NEVER STUCK ON THE SIDELINES, JUST A GUARD
WHEN THINGS GET TOUGH, WHEN THINGS GET HARD
I WILL KEEP HIM CLOSE AT HAND
IN A TEAM
SIDE BY SIDE
THAT'S EXACTLY WHAT I'LL DO
WHEN I AM A HERO TOO!
Man, I really need to pee.

(Suddenly, a ball with a note tied around it flies in from offstage and bonks **INKY** *in the head.)*

INKY. Ow! Hey! Oh, hey, another note!

(**INKY** *opens the letter. Reading:*)

"Dear Blackjack the Bungler's Stupid Sidekick. I have your friend and the Princess. They are my prisoners and I intend to do terrible and mean things to them with my latest invention. Then I intend to take over the world. There is nothing you can do to stop me. So don't even try. I mean it. Don't. It won't work. Don't even think about trying to stop me. You're thinking about it, aren't you? Oh, fiddlesticks. Well then, try and stop me if you can, Super Zero! I'll just capture you too and then no one will be left to stop me! The Kingdom will be mine! MUHUHAHAHA– (*flips the note*) –HAHAHAHA!!! Signed, the Evil Sorcerer Slurm."

(*beat*)

Wow, he really wrote out "MUHUHAHAHAHAHAHAHA!" That's weird.

(*beat*)

Oh no! They captured Blackjack! I have to help him! But how? I'm not a Superhero. Blackjack is, and he got captured. I'm just a sidekick. What do I do?

(**INKY** *starts to pace and plays to the audience for this.*)

I don't think I can do this. I can't go rescue them by myself...but I have to. I'm sure Blackjack would come save me if I was in trouble. I won't let him down, and no one deserves to be Slurm's prisoner, especially the Princess. She's so nice to me. I have to try. If I don't try to save them, who will. I have to give it my best shot. (*to audience*) What do you think? Do you think I can do it? Are you with me? ...All right, let's go!

(**INKY** *prepares to leave.*)

Super Sidekick Inky...AWAY!!!

(**INKY** *exits.*)

SCENE VI

(**INKY** *stands in the entrance to the Caves of Doom.*)

INKY. Ah, here's the cave! Wow, it *is* dark in there. (**INKY** *cautiously sticks his foot into the cave in a fashion that is reminiscent of putting one's toes in a tub of water to check how hot it is.*) Well, that's not so bad!

(**INKY** *enters the cave.*)

Oh, it's dark in here. Really, really dark. Oh wow, I don't know how I'm going to do this. Wait! What did Blackjack always say to himself whenever he went into someplace dark and scary? Oh yeah! "Inky, you go first!"…No, wait, that's not it…after that…what else did he say? Oh yeah! "Pfft! I'm not afraid of the dark!" Let's see if that works.

*(MUSIC: "**THE CAVES OF DOOM**")*

INKY.

I'M NOT AFRAID OF THE DARK

(scary sound effect – owl hooting, wolf howling, etc.)

I'M NOT AFRAID OF THE DARK

(sound effect)

IT MAY CRAWL WITH BEASTS THAT GROWL
THINGS THAT GRUNT AND FIENDS THAT HOWL
BUT THEY'RE JUST SOUNDS, AND SOUNDS CAN'T LEAVE A
    MARK

I WON'T BE SCARED OF THE NIGHT

(sound effect)

ALTHOUGH I COULD USE A SMALL LIGHT

(sound effect)

I MAY FEEL SHIVERS ALONG MY SPINE
BUT THERE'S NO REASON TO THINK I WON'T BE FINE

NO NEED TO WORRY ABOUT CAVERN-DWELLING TROLLS
OR VAMPIRES WHO EAT FRICASSEE OF SOULS
OR ANGRY ANCIENT DRAGONS WHO BREATHE SCORCHING
    JETS OF FLAME

OR MINOTAURS OR DINOSAURS OR HORRORS WITH NO
    NAME
OR HUMAN-EATING DEMONS WHO CAN FLY WITH GIANT
    BAT WINGS AND WHO HAVE THE HEADS OF LIZARDS AND
    THE FRONT TEETH OF A SHARK, BECAUSE...
I'M NOT AFRAID OF THE DARK

(sound effect)

I'M NOT AFRAID OF THE DARK

(sound effect)

IT MIGHT BE QUITE CREEPY HERE
BUT ALL TRUE HEROES PERSEVERE
I CAN'T BE SPOOKED BY EVERY BUMP OR BARK

(sound effect)

'CAUSE THEY'RE JUST SOUNDS, AND SOUNDS CAN'T LEAVE
    A MARK

(A cavalcade of scary sounds comes from the darkness.)

INKY. *(to audience)* I could use a little help here. You guys
wanna help me out? Okay, here we go!

(prompts audience to sing along after each line)

I'M NOT AFRAID OF THE DARK!
I'M NOT AFRAID OF THE DARK!
    I'M NOT AFRAID OF THE DARK!

(The monster sounds intensify.)

Okay, I think I'd better take it from here. Here I go!
Wish me luck!

*(sung while running in place to simulate a mad dash
through the caves:)*

I'M NOT AFRAID OF THE DARK!
I'M NOT AFRAID OF THE DARK!
I'M NOT AFRAID OF THE DARK!
    I'M NOT AFRAID OF THE DARK!

*(***INKY*** *continues running, while monsters swirl around
him, taunting, being scary, and hamming it up. At one
point a* **TINY MONSTER** *bites onto* **INKY***'s arm. This*

might be a clip with googly eyes, or some other simple object. [Not a person.] **INKY** *is oblivious to this tiny assault. Eventually the monsters recede, leaving Inky alone.)*

INKY. *(breathing heavily)* Hey…wait a minute…I think it's a little lighter in here. And the monsters are gone…and they didn't even touch me!

*(***INKY*** notices the* **TINY MONSTER** *clipped to his arm. He flings it offstage.)*

TINY MONSTER VOICE. *(offstage)* Ow!

INKY. And they didn't even touch me! Even though I was pretty scared, I made it!

(Unbeknownst to **INKY,** *the other* **MONSTERS** *emerge behind him, listening in.)*

You know, I think I've discovered one of the secrets of being a hero. It's okay to be afraid, as long as you keep going.

(The other **MONSTERS** *look at each other, considering this. They nod in agreement.)*

AS LONG AS YOU GET WHERE YOU SET OUT TO GO
AND AS LONG AS YOU DO WHAT YOU NEED TO
AS LONG AS YOU DON'T PUT YOUR MISSION ASIDE AND
    YOU'RE STILL THERE AT END OF THE DAY
THEN A LITTLE FEAR OF DARKNESS
JUST A LITTLE FEAR OF DARKNESS
YES, A LITTLE FEAR OF DARKNESS IS OKAY!

(The **MONSTERS** *advance, taking over the next chorus.* **INKY** *freezes, petrified with the realization that he's surrounded.)*

MONSTERS.

THEN A LITTLE FEAR OF DARKNESS
JUST A LITTLE FEAR OF DARKNESS
YES, A LITTLE FEAR OF DARKNESS…

(A **SOLOIST MONSTER** *steps up.)*

SOLOIST MONSTER. *(in a Bluesey, bringing-the-house-down solo)*
IS OKAAAAAAAAAAAAAAAAAAAAAAAAAAAY!!!!!

(The **SOLOIST MONSTER** *bows as the other* **MONSTERS** *cheer, applaud, pat him/her on the back, etc. They march offstage, quite satisfied with their own performance.)*

*(***INKY** *recovers, only to see two* **NINJA KOALAS** *enter! They don't seem to have noticed him…yet.)*

INKY. Uh oh! It's the Ninja Koalas! What do I do? Hmmm…
Oh! I have an idea!

*(***INKY** *reaches into his cloak and pulls out two branches of eucalyptus.)*

I know what Koalas like. Eucalyptus leaves!

*(***INKY** *walks boldly towards the* **NINJA KOALAS***. The* **NINJA KOALAS** *strike fighting poses and look as scary as koala bears wearing Ninja outfits can. They lunge for* **INKY***, but freeze when he holds out the Eucalyptus leaves. They look at one another and greedily grab for the snack.* **INKY** *turns back to the audience and smiles. The* **KOALAS** *greedily snack on the Eucalyptus as* **INKY** *sneaks by them. When the* **KOALAS** *finish, they turn back to where* **INKY** *was and, upon realizing that he's escaped, chase after him.)*

SCENE VII

(Inside the Caves of Doom. Lights up on the **PRINCESS**. *She's shackled to a pillar and reaching out towards a large red button on another pillar nearby labeled "MANACLE RELEASE." Just as she's reaching it, the* **NINJA KOALAS** *enter.)*

*(MUSIC: **"THE PRINCESS ESCAPES"** [underscore])*

(The **PRINCESS** *pulls back and pretends to be helpless. The* **KOALAS** *watch her intently at first, but soon grow bored. They can start playing games, doing martial arts, etc. While they're distracted, the* **PRINCESS** *manages to reach out and hit the button. Suddenly free, she darts offstage. Seeing this, the* **NINJA KOALAS** *make chase.)*

(After a beat, **INKY** *runs in. He has just escaped the* **NINJA KOALAS** *that were chasing him.)*

INKY. Whew! That was close! *(**INKY** notices the pillar.)* Oh, what's this?

*(**INKY** goes to examine the manacles. When he does, the* **PRINCESS** *creeps back onstage with a large rock in her hands. She's about to hit* **INKY***, but, sensing danger, he turns around at the last second.)*

INKY. Ha ha! *(beat)* Princess Penelope?!?

PRINCESS. Inky?!?

INKY. What are you doing? I thought you were chained up!

PRINCESS. I got out of my chains.

INKY. How?

PRINCESS. Slurm told me to just ignore the giant red button right here.

INKY. You mean the one that says "Manacle Release"?

PRINCESS. Yep, that's the one. Might have missed it, too, if he hadn't said anything. So, I hit it and I hid when I heard you coming. I thought you were one of them! I was going to bonk the Ninja Koalas on the head with this rock and escape! What are you doing here?

INKY. I'm here to rescue you!

PRINCESS. Rescue me? Oh, that's so sweet!

INKY. Yeah, but you're already free. Some super sidekick I am. I can't even rescue a Princess right.

PRINCESS. Well, you tried to rescue me, and if I wasn't already free, you would have. That makes you a super-hero, in my book!

INKY. Really?

PRINCESS. Yes, really! And how did you ever get past the Ninja Koalas? They're very dangerous, you know!

INKY. I fed them eucalyptus and then snuck by them and locked them out!

PRINCESS. You fed the bears?

INKY. Yes.

PRINCESS. Oh Inky, what a terrible example! For the kids!

(*indicates the audience*)

INKY. Oh, it's okay, Princess.

PRINCESS. No, it's not okay. Feeding bears is dangerous business! Especially koala bears that are also Ninjas! You could have been hurt!

INKY. (*suitably admonished*) You're right. (*addresses the audience*) Um, children? Please remember: It's okay for me to feed bears, especially koala bears that are Ninjas because I'm a trained super sidekick.

PRINCESS. Hero.

INKY. I'm a trained superher – ...(*realizing what the* **PRINCESS** *just said*)...hero?

(*The* **PRINCESS** *nods.*)

I'm a trained...superhero, but you shouldn't ever do it yourselves. It's very, very dangerous. Okay? Everyone understand? Don't feed the bears. Say it with me now.

(**INKY** *encourages the audience to repeat it with him.*)

Don't feed the bears. (*turns back to the* **PRINCESS**) There. That should do it.

PRINCESS. Spoken like a true superhero.

INKY. Thank you.

(They regard each other, shyly.)

*(MUSIC: "**INKY AND THE PRINCESS**")*

PRINCESS. So…are we…um, ready to make our escape?

INKY. Um, yeah. I…uh, I just need to…*(moves downstage to one side)*

PRINCESS. Right, and I need to…um…grab my…

(The **PRINCESS** *moves downstage to the opposite side.* **INKY** *and the* **PRINCESS** *are smitten with one another. They both steal glances at each other, and become flush with embarrassment whenever their eyes meet.)*

INKY.

> HAVE YOU EVER LIKED A GIRL
> SO MUCH, IT FELT LIKE YOU JUST ATE A BRICK?
> HAS YOUR HEAD BEGUN TO WHIRL
> UNTIL YOU STARTED GETTING MOTION SICK?
> HAVE YOU FELT YOUR STOMACH JUMP?
> YOUR BRAIN BECOME A LUMP?
> YOUR TONGUE FEEL THICK AND FAT?
> I THINK I LIKE A GIRL ABOUT AS MUCH AS THAT

PRINCESS.

> HAVE YOU EVER LIKED A BOY
> SO MUCH, YOUR STOMACH SEEMED TO TURN TO GOO?
> AND FELT LIGHT-HEADED, OUT OF BREATH
> AND EVERY MAJOR SYMPTOM OF THE FLU?
> HAVE YOU FELT YOUR MIND GO NUMB?
> YOUR FINGERS TURN TO GUM?
> YOUR HEART JUMP IN YOUR HAT?
> I JUST MAYBE LIKE A BOY ABOUT AS MUCH AS THAT

INKY.

> EACH TIME SHE'S NEAR IT'S LIKE I DRANK MILK THAT
>   EXPIRED LAST JULY

PRINCESS.

> AND WHEN HE'S HERE IT'S LIKE MY LUNGS HAVE SIMPLY
>   LOST THEIR AIR SUPPLY

INKY & PRINCESS.

I'D TELL [HIM/HER] HOW I FEEL
BUT I'M NOT QUITE SURE HOW [S]HE WOULD REPLY

INKY.

HAVE YOU EVER LIKE A GIRL
    SO MUCH THAT IT…

(half-spoken in a patter)

FELT LIKE A GIANT USED YOUR HEART AS A BOWLING BALL,
    THEN BOWLED A SPARE, THEN PICKED UP THE BALL
    AGAIN, MISSED, AND STARTING JUGGLING THE BALL

(sung normally)

SPINNING IT ROUND AND ROUND?

PRINCESS.

HAVE YOU EVER LIKED A BOY
    SO MUCH…

(half-spoken in a patter)

THAT IT FELT LIKE HUMONGOUS SPIDERS CAUGHT
    YOU IN A WEB AND STARTED USING YOUR BODY AS A
    TRAMPOLINE, THEN IN MID-JUMP DECIDED THEY WERE
    BORED AND WENT OUT FOR ICE CREAM, LEAVING YOU
    HANGING THERE

(sung normally)

ALONE AND UPSIDE DOWN?

INKY & PRINCESS.

HAVE YOU FELT A TRIFLE SCARED?
AND BODILY IMPAIRED?
LIKE YOUR HEART WAS IN A CLUTCH?
I JUST MAYBE LIKE SOMEONE
APPROXIMATELY THAT MUCH

(By the end of the song, they're within arms reach of one another, still looking at each other shyly. The music fades out. Beat. They both look like they're about to say something when, from out of nowhere, a cry for help echoes through the cave.)

PRINCESS. Oh no! Slurm must have captured another Princess!

INKY. Oh, no. That's just Blackjack. *(beat)* Blackjack! He's here! Oh my gosh! I almost forgot! Slurm has him!

PRINCESS. Well, let's go save him, then!

INKY. Wait, *I'm* the one who's supposed to rescue him.

PRINCESS. What, you're telling me I can't come along and help? Is it because I'm a Princess? Is it because I'm a girl? I swear, I am so tired of you boys telling me all the time what I can and can't do simply because I'm a girl. I can be just as good a hero as the rest of you, you know.

INKY. It's just that…

PRINCESS. What?

*(MUSIC: "**SUPERHEROES AWAY!**" [underscore])*

INKY. It's just that…I don't want you to get hurt. I like you.

*(The **PRINCESS** is taken aback.)*

PRINCESS. Oh! How sweet!

*(The **PRINCESS** gives **INKY** a kiss on the cheek.)*

For luck. *(beat)* I like you too, and I promise I won't get hurt if you don't get hurt either, okay?

INKY. Okay.

(They strike a Superhero Flying Pose.)

BOTH. Superheroes AWAY!

(exit)

SCENE VIII

(Another column with a giant red button and a sign saying "DO NOT TOUCH" stands stage right. BLACKJACK is chained to the other pillar, stage left, in a single pool of light. The rest of the stage is dark.)

BLACKJACK. Hello? Is there anybody out there? Just shout if you can hear me! *(sung a la Pink Floyd's* Comfortably Numb*)* Is there anyone home?

(SLURM enters in darkness, goggles over his eyes.)

SLURM. I can hear you, hero, and I will be the last one ever to hear you as you cry for mercy.

(SLURM claps twice. The lights come up fully in the cave. He howls in pain as the sudden brightening in the room hurts his eyes through his night-vision goggles. He pulls the goggles off his face as quickly as he can. BLACKJACK observes this and tries not to laugh.)

BLACKJACK. *(beat, sarcastic)* Oh. Please. Don't hurt me.

SLURM. Oh, you will beg, hero. You will beg when I unleash my latest invention upon you.

BLACKJACK. Your latest invention? As if the banana peel plot wasn't pathetic enough. What are you going to do now, tickle me to death?

(SLURM is stunned.)

SLURM. How did you know?!? Have you been reading my evil villain's handbook?

BLACKJACK. How did I know what?

SLURM. About my latest secret weapon? How did you know?!? WHO TOLD YOU??? NINJA KOALAS?!?

BLACKJACK. Um…you did.

SLURM. I did?

BLACKJACK. Yes. Just now.

SLURM. *(beat, realizing)* BLAST IT! You and your superhero trickery! But it's all for naught, Blackjack the Bold!

(SFX: "Blackjack's Chime")

*(**BLACKJACK** and **SLURM** turn to the audience for a beat and each give a large, toothy grin.)*

SLURM. *(cont.)* It's time for you to meet your doom! First you, then the Kingdom! All will tremble before my might when I wield the…

*(**SLURM** reaches under his coat. What he's looking for isn't there. He remembers where it is and claps twice. The lights onstage go out.)*

No! That's the lights.

*(**SLURM** claps twice again. The lights come back on. Beat. He claps three times. A **NINJA KOALA** enters with a Terrible Tickler. He takes it from them and brandishes the giant feather.)*

TERRIBLE TICKLER!!!

*(MUSIC: **"TERRIBLE TICKLER FANFARE"** [underscore])*

BLACKJACK. You're going to torture me…with a feather?

SLURM. Yes.

BLACKJACK. A feather.

SLURM. Well…it's quite a terrible feather.

BLACKJACK. Puh-lease, Slurm. This scheme is pathetic. Even for you. It'll never work.

SLURM. Never work, eh? Think you could come up with something better?

BLACKJACK. Of course! I'm sure I could come up with a hundred better schemes than that.

SLURM. Oh yeah?

BLACKJACK. Yeah.

SLURM. Like what, Mr. Smarty Superhero?

BLACKJACK. Like…hmmm… How about…um…maybe… No. Wow…it must be hard to be evil.

SLURM. My point exactly. No one understands my art.

(MUSIC: "SLURM'S SOLILOQUY")

SLURM.

> YOU MIGHT THINK A MAN IN MY POSITION'S GOT IT MADE
> THAT CONQUERING A KINGDOM IS A BREEZE
> THAT ONLY SHOWS YOU'RE UNACQUAINTED WITH THE
>   TRIALS OF MY TRADE
> FOR THE EVIL LIFE IS NEVER FILLED WITH EASE
>
> PERHAPS YOU THINK IT'S SIMPLE TO BE VILLAINOUS AND
>   VILE
> THAT ONE NEVER HAS TO HONE ONE'S BITE OR BARK
> IN TRUTH I TAKE GREAT PAINS TO GET MY ILL-BEGOTTEN
>   GAINS
> TO BE SINISTER IS NO STALK IN THE PARK!
>
> IT'S HARD TO BE EVIL
> IT'S TOUGH TO BE MEAN
> YOU DON'T SIMPLY TAKE A TONIC AND THE NEXT DAY BE
>   DEMONIC
> IT'S A NEVER-ENDING FIGHT
> IT'S A ROUND-THE-CLOCK REGIME
> IT'S WORK TO BE WICKED
> OR TO MAKE ONE PERSON SAD
> TO DISRUPT THE COMMON WEAL CAN BE SO VERY
>   DIFFICILE
> AND THERE'S PRECIOUS LITTLE GUIDANCE TO BE HAD
> IT'S REALLY RATHER TRICKY TO BE BAD
>
> HAVE YOU EVER TRIED TO DETONATE A TRAIN?

(spoken aside:) Well? Have you?

> IT'S NOT AS STRAIGHT AND EASY AS THE STORIES MAKE IT
>   SOUND
> YOU'VE GOT TO LAY EXPLOSIVES OVER EVERY INCH OF
>   GROUND
> AND TO READ THE SCHEDULE RIGHT – OR YOU'LL JUST
>   WASTE DYNAMITE
> HAVE YOU EVER TRIED TO BREAK INTO A BANK?

(spoken aside:) Didn't think so!

> IF YOU THINK IT'S SIMPLY DONE THEN YOU ARE IN FOR
>   QUITE A SHOCK

YOU'VE GOT TO BRIBE THE GUARD, THEN SPEND AN HOUR
  WITH A LOCK
AND GOOD LUCK AVOIDING HARM IF SOMEONE SETS OFF
  THE ALARM!

IT'S HARD TO BE EVIL
IT'S TOUGH TO BE MEAN
YOU CAN'T SIMPLY READ A BOOK AND CULTIVATE A
  THREATENING LOOK
YOU'LL BE TIRED AND AFRAID
IT'S AS BAD AS SECOND GRADE!
IT'S WORK TO BE WICKED
COMPLEX TO BE A CAD
YOU'LL HAVE TO LEARN TO WORK A FLOG, LEST YOU JUST
  BE A JERK-IN-PROGRESS
AND AN UNTRAINED ANTIHERO'S SIMPLY SAD
IT'S REALLY QUITE EXHAUSTING TO BE BAD

HAVE YOU EVER TRIED TO KIDNAP SOMEONE FAMOUS?
WELL THE PROCESS WILL ADD TEN YEARS TO YOUR AGE!
YOU HAVE TO RENT A LAIR AND BUY AIR FRESHENER FOR
  THE CAGE
AND IT REALLY GETS MY GOAT WHEN I MISSPELL A RANSOM
  NOTE!

AND KOALAS!

(spoken aside:) Don't get me started.

THOSE AUSSIES ARE JUST CONSTANT AGGRAVATION
FOR ONE THING, THEY'RE A GIANT PAIN TO GET PAST
  IMMIGRATION
AND HOW I WISH THEY'D SHIPPED US SOME SUPPLIES OF
  EUCALYPTUS!

IT'S HARD TO BE EVIL
FATIGUING TO BE FOUL
YOU CAN'T SIMPLY GRAB A MASK AND SOME
  MELODRAMATIC COWL
YOU'VE MUST CAUSE CALAMITY
OR AT LEAST A "WOE-IS-ME"!
IT'S WORK TO BE WICKED
IT'S ENOUGH TO DRIVE YOU MAD

YOU THINK YOUR JOB IS HARD?
YOU'RE NEVER RUNNING FROM THE GUARDS!
AND IF YOU'VE NEVER SEEN A DUNGEON, THEN BE GLAD
IT'S VERY VERY TRICKY TO BE BAD

NINJA KOALAS.

IT'S HARD TO BE EVIL!

SLURM. Ever try stealing candy from a baby? They bite!

NINJA KOALAS.

IT'S HARD TO BE EVIL!

SLURM. How can I set forest fires when tinder is so expensive?

NINJA KOALAS.

IT'S HARD TO BE EVIL!

SLURM. You try wearing black all the time!

NINJA KOALAS.

IT'S HARD TO BE EVIL!

SLURM. Don't get me started about the insurance!

NINJA KOALAS.

IT'S HARD TO BE EVIL!

SLURM. All the good slogans are gone!

SLURM & NINJA KOALAS.

IT'S VERY VERY VERY VERY VERY VERY TRICKY TO BE BAD!

SLURM. …but it does pay rather nicely!

BLACKJACK. Wow…I see your point.

SLURM. Thank you. Now, where were we? Oh, yes. The Terrible Tickler!

*(MUSIC: **"TERRIBLE TICKLER FANFARE"** [underscore])*

BLACKJACK. You do realize that you can only tickle one person at a time with that. I mean, how are you going to terrorize the whole wide Kingdom with a single feather?

SLURM. The Ninja Koalas will help me.

BLACKJACK. Oh please, those overgrown teddy bears?

SLURM. Koala bears.

BLACKJACK. Whatever. Even if you had a hundred Ninja Koalas, each with a Terrible Tickler, you still couldn't tickle everyone in the Kingdom!

SLURM. Oh, you misunderstand, hero. Always thinking about things the wrong way. I don't have to tickle everyone, just the right one. The Queen. I'm going to tickle the Queen until she turns the throne over to me!

BLACKJACK. Oh, yeah, right. Like that'll really work.

SLURM. Don't believe me? I bet I can make you beg me to stop. You'll offer me anything I want.

BLACKJACK. Sure. Like that will happen.

SLURM. Very well, hero. Have it your way.

(**SLURM** *starts to tickle* **BLACKJACK**'s *torso with the feather.* **BLACKJACK** *tries to resist but can't hold in the laughter. It grows until it explodes out of him. Finally…*)

BLACKJACK. Stop! Stop! I'll give you anything you want! Just stop!

(**SLURM** *stops.*)

SLURM. Haha! Success! You see, hero? Not even you could withstand the might of one Terrible Tickler! The Queen will never be able to resist the Ninja Koalas and I when we use THREE on her!

(**SLURM** *produces two more Terrible Ticklers!*)

BLACKJACK. You monster!

SLURM. Thank you!

BLACKJACK. You'll never get away with this! Inky and I will stop you!

SLURM. That's where you're wrong. You're here, chained to the wall. Your pathetic little sidekick is still standing out in a dark field doing a pee-pee dance because you told him to wait and hunt for Snipes! Snipes! Seriously? Everyone knows they don't exist!

BLACKJACK. They don't?

SLURM. Of course they don't! Everyone knows that! My Ninja Koalas will make short work of him. Your pride is your folly, Blackjack the Bold, and there will be no happy ending for you. I'm going to tickle you to DEATH!

(**SLURM** *begins to tickle* **BLACKJACK. BLACKJACK** *laughs uncontrollably.*)

(Blackout)

SCENE IX

(Elsewhere in the Caves of Doom. **INKY** *and the* **PRINCESS** *enter.* **BLACKJACK**'s *laughter can still be heard in the distance.)*

INKY. Oh no! Do you hear that? Blackjack's really in trouble!

PRINCESS. Well come on then! We've got to save him!

INKY. ...I don't think I can do this. I don't think I can do this! It's one thing to overcome my fear of the dark, but this...this is a Hero's work. And look what happened to the last hero that tried! I mean, I'm only a sidekick. Maybe we should go back to town and see if the Queen can send some guards to help or something.

(He begins to edge towards the exit.)

PRINCESS. Inky! No! We don't have time for that. You're it. *We're* it! You and I have to save him. There's no other choice.

INKY. But–

PRINCESS. Inky, listen to me. You can do this. I know you can.

*(MUSIC: **"THE FINAL ENCOUNTER: PART 1"**)*

EVERY ONCE UPON A TIME THERE COMES A TIME
WHEN THE HOURGLASS STARTS RUNNING OUT OF SAND
AS THE VILLAINS START APPROACHING VICTORY
AND ALMOST SEEM TO HAVE THE UPPER HAND
LISTEN HARD, YOU'LL HEAR THE DISTANT BATTLE CALL
AND THE EVER-LOUDER POUNDING OF THE DRUMS
ALL THE SIGNS ARE POINTING TO...
WELL, I GUESS, ME AND YOU
SO PUT YOUR BRAVE FACE ON, 'CAUSE HERE THEY COME!

IT'S THE FINAL ENCOUNTER
IT'S THE LAST CONFRONTATION
IT'S THE CALL TO GET CLEVER
IN A TOUGH SITUATION

IT ALL COMES DOWN TO THIS
NOT A MOMENT TO LOSE
DRAW A LINE IN THE SAND
AND IGNITE ALL THE FLARES

TIME TO CASH IN THE CHIPS
TIME TO CALL IN THE TROOPS
AND COME UP WITH A PLAN
THAT'S MUCH BETTER THAN THEIRS
IT'S THE END OF THE MISSION
THERE'S NO ENCOUNTER AFTER THIS ONE

INKY. Okay. Let's go. I–I can do this.

PRINCESS. We can do this together.

INKY. Together. Let's go do some rescuing!

SCENE X

(Back to **BLACKJACK***'s cell.* **BLACKJACK** *is still being tickled by* **SLURM**. **BLACKJACK** *is exhausted from hysterical laughter.* **INKY** *and the* **PRINCESS** *enter.)*

INKY. Not so fast!

BLACKJACK. Inky!

SLURM. Sidekick!

INKY. Blackjack!

BLACKJACK. Princess!

SLURM. Ninja Koalas!

(Enter the **NINJA KOALAS**, *each wielding a Terrible Tickler.)*

PRINCESS. Ninja Koalas!

(The **NINJA KOALAS** *bark, grunt or make some other sort of short, menacing sound.)*

(The **NINJA KOALAS** *flank* **INKY** *and the* **PRINCESS**.*)*

INKY. *(to* **PRINCESS***)* I think we're outnumbered.

BLACKJACK. Inky! Princess! Save yourselves! It's too late for me!

INKY. Don't worry Blackjack! I'm a hero now! I'll save you!

BLACKJACK. You're a hero?!? Since when???

PRINCESS. Since he saved me!

BLACKJACK. YOU saved the Princess?

INKY. Well, I kinda did.

BLACKJACK. That's my job!

PRINCESS. Never mind whose job it was to save me when! What are we going to do now?

SLURM. Nothing! It's too late, sidekick! Your hero is doomed! Then, there will be no one left to stop me!

*(***SLURM** *starts to tickle* **BLACKJACK**.*)*

INKY. We have to do something! Quick!

PRINCESS. Inky, you stop Slurm. I've got the Ninja Koalas.

INKY. Are you sure? They're very dangerous, you know.

PRINCESS. Are you saying I can't beat them because I'm a girl?

INKY. No.

PRINCESS. Good, because otherwise, I'd have to kick your butt.

INKY. Okay. Just remember, you promised not to get hurt.

PRINCESS. So did you. Now, go save Blackjack!

INKY. Okay!

>*(The **PRINCESS** dives towards stage right and whips out some eucalyptus leaves.)*

PRINCESS. Okay you overgrown fur balls, come and get me!

>*(The **NINJA KOALAS** see the eucalyptus, drop their Terrible Ticklers, and run after her.)*

INKY. Wow, I guess they have a one-track mind…

>*(**BLACKJACK** is laughing hysterically.)*

BLACKJACK. *(through fits of laughter)* A little help here?!?

INKY. Wha–? Oh yeah!

>*(**INKY** looks around the room for something to use. He spots a discarded Terrible Tickler, tumbles over to it and jumps up, wielding the feather like a rapier.)*

En garde!

SLURM. What? Oh, so the little sidekick wants to play hero now, eh?

INKY. That's where you're wrong, Slurm. I am a hero, like my best friend before me.

SLURM. Oh please. Enough of the thinly-veiled movie references. Let's just end this already!

>*(**INKY** and **SLURM** begin to duel during the song.)*

>*(MUSIC: "**THE FINAL ENCOUNTER: PART 2**")*

SLURM.
> SILLY LITTLE BOY, AT LAST YOUR TIME HAS COME
> YOU HAVE MEDDLED IN MY PLANS FOR FAR TOO LONG
> IF YOU'VE COME THIS WAY EXPECTING VICTORY
> THEN PLEASE ALLOW ME TO REVEAL HOW WRONG…
>   YOU ARE
> EVERY FABLE HAS A FINAL CHAPTER
> AND EVERY DRAMA HAS A CLOSING ACT
> YOU'VE HAD FUN PRETENDING, BUT I'M SORRY –
>   PLAYTIME'S ENDING!
> IT'S THE GRAND FINALE, OR TO BE EXACT
>
> IT'S YOUR FINAL ENCOUNTER
> IT'S YOUR LAST CONFRONTATION
> IT'S YOUR TERMINAL SHOWDOWN
> AND IMPENDING CREMATION
>
> IT'S THE END OF THE LINE
> IT'S THE PART WHERE YOU LOSE
> TIME TO CEASE AND DESIST
> AND CONCLUDE YOUR AFFAIRS
> TELL YOUR LOVED ONES GOODBYE
> SIGN YOUR NAME ON YOUR WILL
> BLOW US ALL ONE LAST KISS
> AND PRONOUNCE ANY PRAYERS
> AND ACCEPT YOUR POSITION
> YOU'VE NO ENCOUNTERS AFTER THIS ONE

> *(The duel brings* **INKY** *and* **SLURM** *over to the giant red button.* **INKY** *sees it.)*

INKY. *(while fighting)* Hey Slurm, what does that giant red button do?

SLURM. You mean the giant red button over there that releases your friend from his chains? Oh, nothing. Nothing at all.

INKY. Oh, okay. *(beat)* Hey! Wait a minute!

> *(***INKY*** *breaks off the fight and bolts over to the giant red button. He hits it and* **BLACKJACK** *is freed!)*

BLACKJACK. At last! *(***BLACKJACK*** *hops up and grabs a third Terrible Tickler.)* Have at thee!

SLURM. Blast you, sidekick! How did you know?!?

INKY. You told me!

SLURM. What?

BLACKJACK. Remind me to invite him to our next poker game.

SLURM. Never mind that, you super zeroes. I am a master of the Terrible Tickler.

*(MUSIC: **"TERRIBLE TICKLER FANFARE"** [underscore]. This is interrupted by the next line.)*

(to the pit/booth) NOT NOW! *(**SLURM** turns back to the heroes.)* You'll never beat me! Have at you!

*(MUSIC: **"BATTLE WITH SLURM"** [underscore])*

*(**SLURM** engages both **INKY** and **BLACKJACK** in a duel, fighting back and forth. During the fight, **SLURM** bonks **BLACKJACK** on the head. **BLACKJACK** falls and does not get up.)*

INKY. Blackjack!

*(**INKY** and **SLURM** are standing right beside the wall manacles. They cross feathers and disarm one another. **SLURM** grapples **INKY** and they engage in the "test of strength." **SLURM** is winning. The **PRINCESS** reenters.)*

PRINCESS. Inky!

INKY. Princess! Help!

PRINCESS. You can do it, Inky!

INKY. Princess! I can't hold on much longer!

PRINCESS. Keep it up, Inky! We believe in you! Don't we, everyone?

*(The **PRINCESS** turns to the audience for help and encouragement.)*

C'mon everyone! Cheer for Inky!

*(Empowered by the cheering, **INKY** slowly overwhelms **SLURM** and forces him against the wall. **BLACKJACK** slowly gets up.)*

INKY. Blackjack! Hit the giant red button!

> (**BLACKJACK** *hits the giant red button and* **SLURM** *is chained to the wall! All is saved!*)

SLURM. NOOOOOOOOOOO!!!! Foiled again!

INKY. We did it!

BLACKJACK. Great job, Inky! I couldn't have done it without you. All right, Princess, let's get you properly rescued and back home.

PRINCESS. What?

BLACKJACK. Come on, you know the routine. The hero rescues the Princess and is adored by the Kingdom and rewarded handsomely with a kiss. Pucker up.

PRINCESS. Okay, I'll reward my hero.

> (*The* **PRINCESS** *goes and plants a big kiss on* **INKY**'s *cheek.*)

My hero.

BLACKJACK. What? How can that be? He's just a sidekick!

PRINCESS. Inky overcame his fear of the dark. Inky beat the Ninja Koalas. Inky rescued me AND he rescued you. Inky beat Slurm in a Terrible Tickler duel while you were taking a nap and he stopped Slurm's evil plot! And all this after you left him alone on a Snipe Hunt. A Snipe Hunt?!? Really?!? Snipes don't even exist!

INKY. They don't?

PRINCESS. *(still in* **BLACKJACK**'s *face)* Of course they don't!

INKY. I knew that.

PRINCESS. *(still to* **BLACKJACK***)* EVERYBODY knows that! Now, Inky is my hero and you'd better treat him like it. Got it?

SLURM. *(aside, to* **INKY***)* She's terrifying!

INKY. *(aside, to* **SLURM***)* I know.

BLACKJACK. Oh, I suppose you're right. Inky! Front and center!

> (**INKY** *moves to* **BLACKJACK.***)

From this day forth, you'll no longer be my sidekick.

INKY. What? But Blackjack...I thought I...

BLACKJACK. You'll be my partner. I'm promoting you to full hero status as of now.

INKY. Really?

BLACKJACK. Really.

(**BLACKJACK** *and* **INKY** *shake hands.* **INKY** *and the* **PRINCESS** *hug.*)

EPILOGUE

*(MUSIC: **"HAPPILY EVER AFTER"** [underscore])*

*(The **NARRATOR** re-enters with her storybook tucked under her arm.)*

NARRATOR. And so it happened. Inky became a hero. He, the Princess and Blackjack returned to the Queen with a captured Slurm in tow. The Queen was SO grateful.

*(**INKY** and **BLACKJACK** take the same positions from Scene 1 in the Courtroom. The **NARRATOR** once again assumes the mantle of the **QUEEN**.)*

QUEEN. I'm SO grateful! Superhero Inky, in gratitude for your unparalleled show of bravery and goodness in saving the Kingdom once again from another evil plot, we hereby award you our highest honor – the Bronze Coconut Medallion with Crossed Licorice Bars. May you wear it proudly.

INKY. Thank you, your Highness.

*(The **QUEEN** becomes the **NARRATOR** again. She moves stage right and re-opens her storybook.)*

NARRATOR. Inky and Blackjack fought evil as partners together from that day forward.

*(**INKY** and **BLACKJACK** strike hero poses together.)*

Slurm was locked away forever, never to be seen or heard from again.

SLURM. *(still captive)* Wait, what?

NARRATOR. The Queen had a special form of justice in mind for him: poetic.

*(**NINJA KOALAS** enter with Terrible Ticklers and escort **SLURM** off while tickling him.)*

ALL. And they all lived happily ever after.

*(The **CITIZENS** from the prologue enter, carrying signs and pictures of Inky. They swarm him for autographs. **INKY** loves the attention. A reprise of Blackjack's theme starts.)*

*(MUSIC: "**SUPER FINALE**")*

BLACKJACK.

GOOD DAY!
PERHAPS SOME EVIL FIENDS ARE IN YOUR WAY
AND THEY NEED A LITTLE PERSUASION

INKY.

MAYBE YOU'RE HAVING TROUBLE WITH SOME VILLAINY
OR A DROUGHT OR DRAGON INVASION

ENSEMBLE.

WELL HELP'S A-COMIN' AND THUGS ARE RUNNING
'CAUSE THEY DON'T STACK AGAINST INKY AND BLACKJACK
THEY'LL [WE'LL] JOIN THE FRAY AND THEY'LL [WE'LL]
    SOLVE THE CRIME
AND THEY'LL [WE'LL] SAVE DAY IN THE NICK OF TIME
AS ONLY SUPER CHAMPIONS CAN!

BLACKJACK.

CAUSE A HERO'S HERE –

INKY. Ahem!

THERE ARE TWO HEROES HERE!

BLACKJACK. *(as if remembering:)* Oh yeah!

ENSEMBLE.

OH YEAH!

*(The ensemble strikes a tableau. **INKY** and the **PRINCESS** share a kiss as the lights fade. Pin spot on a **NINJA KOALA** making a "Yucky" face. Another **NINJA KOALA** looks at the heroes kiss, then looks at the yucky face **KOALA** and kisses him on the cheek.)*

(Blachout)